ISBN: 978-1-953177-35-3

Edition: August 2020

For all inquiries, please contact us at:
info@puppysmiles.org

To see more of our books, visit us at:
www.PuppyDogsAndIceCream.com

# This book is given with love

_____

_____

They had wandered too long in the unknown park.

The sun had gone down, and it was getting dark.

As the night fell, the air soon turned cold.

The boy held out his hand for his sister to hold.

"I'm scared," she said, as she looked all around.

"We'll be fine," he said. "Look! See the tracks on the ground?"

There in the snow, there were prints for them to follow.

Where the deer had walked, the snow was now hollow.

So, they started to walk with hoofprints as their guide

To find a place for the night, where they could both hide.

They soon came upon a circle of very tall trees,

The snow was so dense it came up to their knees.


A family of deer walked up close to see

Who these two-legged creatures could possibly be.

They had never seen children, so they wanted to know

Why they were there and stuck in the snow.

"I think those are the deer that made the tracks here.
If we follow where they go, we'll have nothing to fear."
The boy spoke softly, and his sister nodded her head,
They both wished they were home and tucked into bed.

So, they both kept walking and following the deer.
Then, there was a bright light, and the path became clear.
The stars were sparkling gems in the sky
And more animals followed, as the children walked by.

Up ahead in a clearing, shone splendid rays of light...

It was a beautiful church, a beacon in the night.

They looked at God's beauty that was all around,

They forgot they were lost...inner peace was soon found.

The boy said, "Inside the church, we'll be safe and sound,"

But when they got to the entrance, no one was around.

And yet, the place was lit with an angelic light...

It seemed so heavenly, though it was locked up tight.

As they walked to a window, something amazing occurred,

The stained glass was moving and hymns could be heard.

As they slowly looked up, they saw the first story,

It was Christ's first miracle in all of His glory.

A wedding had started, and He was a guest.

Then His Mother, Mary, came and made a request.

"Please help the bride and groom on their special day.

They've run out of wine and are in dismay."

The servers poured water into six jars of stone,

Per Christ's request, then they left them alone.

With a wave of His hand in a miracle Divine,

He turned the plain water into sweet-tasting wine!

"How did Jesus do that?" the wide-eyed girl asked her brother.

The boy said, "By the Grace of God, and to please His Mother.

That's the kind of love I have for Mom and Dad,

Like the hugs they give us even after we are bad.

They walked further down and a new window came into view

With bright rays of light that warmly streamed through.

There they saw Jesus, who was surrounded by a crowd,

As He spoke of God's Kingdom clearly and loud.

Then Christ's disciples came up to Him to speak,
"Lord, we've been here many hours, and the people feel weak.
They are tired and hungry. It's been a very long day.
We can't feed them all, we must send them away."

Jesus asked, "We don't have enough food so they can all stay?"
The disciples replied, "There's not enough to feed 5,000 today."
Jesus said, "Bring what you have to me. This is my wish."
They delivered five loaves of bread and two small fish.

Jesus touched the food, gazed to heaven and prayed,

And soon His God-given powers were proudly displayed.

The disciples began to feed all who were there,

And as the food multiplied, there was plenty to share.


All the people were happy, it was a blessing to each,

They stayed many hours more and listened to Jesus teach.

The boy smiled to his sister, "Jesus gives us what we need.

Just as He fed the hungry crowd, He'll provide if you believe."

The snow began to fall as the children continued to walk.

The miracle of the windows soon silenced their talk.

The third story showed the beginnings of a huge storm.

The disciples were huddled together in a boat to stay warm.

Jesus prayed on the shore as the winds started to blow.

As the storm became stronger, fear began to grow.

Through crashing waves, Jesus ventured out toward the boat,

He walked on the water just like He was on top of a float.

At first the disciples thought they were seeing a ghost, not a man,

But, little did they know, it was part of Christ's plan.

This miracle was about having faith to overcome doubt.

Jesus said, "Don't be afraid. I am your Lord. Just walk out."

Peter bravely said, "I will walk out to you, Lord."

And at the beginning, his courage had soared,

But, he began to sink, as the waves crashed and the wind blew.

Peter became scared, and he didn't know what to do.


He cried out, "Lord, save me! Please give me your hand!"

Jesus grabbed him, but He wanted Peter to understand.

Jesus asked, "What happened? You were walking out to me.

If you'd only kept faith, you could walk, can't you see?"

The girl spoke, "We should have faith that we'll be safe too."

"Yes," said her brother, "Even when it's not easy to do.

What do you think the next story will be?"

They were excited as they walked to the fourth window to see.


The scene came alive, and they saw Jesus entering a city,

Ten lepers approached Him and cried out "Lord, have pity!"

"You shall all be healed," Jesus smiled with emotion,

"Now go to the church and express your devotion."

One of the men rushed back to give thanks he was cured,
"I'm so grateful, Lord, You've made my prayers heard.
It's thanks to You that I'm completely healed."
At Christ's feet, he bowed his head and kneeled.

"Where are the others?" Jesus asked, "You are the only grateful soul?
I thank you for returning. Your faith has made you whole."
The girl looked to her brother, "I'm thankful I'm with you."
"Me too," he smiled, "Giving thanks is what we should do."

A fifth, lively window lit up for the children to view.

They walked further in the snow to a scene marvelous and new.

There were lots of families living their lives day to day.

As they served the Lord at work, at home, and at play.

Then the scene changed, and they suddenly realized,

Their own family was pictured, they couldn't believe their eyes!

The girl smiled. "It's Mom and Dad, and we're even there too."

The boy grinned. "And Jesus is blessing us in this beautiful view."

There was only one window that was left to see.

The children couldn't imagine just what it might be.

A choir sang loudly and a rainbow of light poured through,

From around the world, they saw what Christians do.

All races and nations were gladly helping out

To save others from sickness, from fear, and from doubt.

And as they brought joy, Jesus Christ could be found there,

In every little gesture of kindness and care.

The church doors opened and they saw Mom and Dad.

Their mom hugged them both, "You're safe! We're so glad!"

Their dad smiled, "You know that you shouldn't wander away.

Next time you must stay closer to us when you play."

The girl nodded, "Can we go home now? I can't wait to get in bed."

Their mom laughed, "Yes, honey, you're such a sleepyhead."

"But first," their dad said, "The church doors are open wide.

So let's go say a quick prayer of thanks inside."

The four of them walked in and knelt down in a pew,

And they prayed and gave thanks for all they'd been through.

After getting home, and through years of happiness and laughter,

They remembered the special church forever thereafter.